Fairy Hill

May and the Music Show

by Cari Meister
illustrated by Erika Meza

SCHOLASTIC INC.

For Colette

Text copyright © 2018 by Cari Meister
Illustration copyright © 2018 by Scholastic Inc.

Library of Congress Cataloging-in-Publication Data
Names: Meister, Cari, author. I Meza, Erika, illustrator.
Title: May and the Music Show / by Cari Meister; illustrated by Erika Meza.
Description: New York, NY : Scholastic Inc., [2018] I Series: Fairy Hill [3]; I Summary:
Luna, Ruby, and May are busy practicing for the Fairy Hill music show, and together
they perform beautifully—but when it is time for Luna's solo song she freezes up,
and it is up to May and her bells to help overcome Luna's stage fright.
Identifiers: LCCN 2017020252 I ISBN 9781338121841 (pbk.)
Subjects: LCSH: Fairies—Juvenile fiction. I Magic—Juvenile fiction. I CYAC: Fairies—Fiction.
Performing arts—Fiction. I Stage fright—Fiction. I Friendship—Fiction.
Classification: LCC PZ7.M515916 May 2018
DDC [E]—dc23 LC record available at https://lccn.loc.gov/2017020252

10 9 8 7 6 5 4 3 2 1   18 19 20 21 22

Printed in U.S.A.   40
First printing 2018

Book design by Steve Ponzo

The Fairy Hill music show is tonight!

Luna, Ruby, and May will be in the show.

Luna will sing.

Ruby will play the flute.

May will ring the bells.

It is their first show.

Luna and Ruby are excited!

"I have a big solo," says Luna.

"I cannot wait to sing by myself."

"I cannot wait to be up on stage," says Ruby.

But May is worried.
"I hope I can learn to play the bells in time,"
she says.

"We will help you practice," says Luna.

"Let's go to my house," says Ruby.

The friends fly to Ruby's house.
"Your big wings are so pretty," May tells
her friends.
"I hope I get my big wings soon, too."

"You will!" Luna says.

"The Fairy Queen will visit when you do something brave, kind, or helpful," Ruby says.

The fairies rush inside.

"I am excited for tonight!" says Luna.

"The show will be so fun!" says Ruby.

"I hope so," says May.

May looks at the music.

There is so much to learn!

"Do not worry," says Luna.

"We have lots of time before the show."

The fairies practice all day.

Luna sings.

Ruby plays the flute.

May rings the bells.

"Good work, May!" says Luna.

"We all sound great," says Ruby.

"We are ready!" says May.

It is almost show time!
"Let's fly," says Ruby.
"We do not want to be late."

16

The show is starting!
The fairies are on stage.
They sing and play.
May rings the bells.

The crowd claps.
The fairies bow.

"That was fun!" says May.
"I loved playing the bells!"

The show is not over yet.

"It is time for your solo, Luna!" says Ruby.

"Good luck!" says May.

Luna flutters out on stage.
She opens her mouth to sing.
Nothing comes out!

"Oh no!" says May.
"Luna is too nervous.
She cannot sing!"

May rushes to help.
She lifts her bells.
She plays Luna's song.

It works!

Luna sings along.

Her stage fright is gone!

Luna's song ends.
"Bravo!" the fairies cheer.

Luna hugs her friend.

"Thank you, May," she says.

"I could not have done it without you!"

Ring-a ling-ling! Ring-a ling-ling!
It is the Fairy Queen!

"May," says the Fairy Queen.
"You helped Luna find her voice.
Today you earn your big wings."

The Fairy Queen taps her magic wand.
May's wings grow.
They sparkle and shimmer.

"Your wings are pretty!" says Ruby.

"They shine so bright!" says Luna.

May flies into the air with her friends.
"Now we can fly together!" she says.